MW01228530

Slee
Awake

by

Christopher Smokes Cogar

I Would Like to Thank Everyone for The Feeling of Life You All Have Given Me. Thank you Amber for All That You Do for Me and Continue to Do! My Fans and San Francisco Family, I

Thank You So Much for
The Support. Love You All
So Much! Dedication Page
for All Friends and Family
Who Helped by Donating or
Providing Support Sandra
Cogar (The Best Aunt) Joy
Roman (Funny Aunt) Brian
Gallagher (Fucking Best
Tattoo Artist) Dana Butler
(The Best Artist in The
World) Dave Barnes (Funny
as Fuck) Katie Herska
(True Little Monster)
Damien Patat (Life of The
Party) Marky Moe
(Especially Marky Moe) Kali

(SF) (Badass Punk Ska Biker)

Augustina Westington

(I wouldn't be alive or who I am if it wasn't for you and your faith in me, I'm forever grateful)

Chapter 1: Where It All Started

I've always been a fan of wild adventures but this one I assure you wasn't one I wanted. Over the course of all my writings, you'll find what's left of the person of who I used to be.

2 weeks ago on the night of my birthday. After a crazy night, I figured I might relax a bit. I threw myself on my futon

and decided to start listening to some of the tracks I just made, I listened to one track that got me thinking the track was dreams I can't reach and some of the lyrics made me a little unsure they went like this "I woke up one night in a daze crazed with fear as I noticed these wires attached to my ears I notice men in lab suits with instruments they told me to lie down and concentrate again and that's when I awoke once more to find myself in my bedroom lying on my floor" as I listened I started to remember the dream from that night but the problem was it seemed more real than a dream. So I thought well maybe someone has a theory about this type of matter so I went on a forum and published my dream for public view and to receive comments to see if anyone else had a similar dream and this is when it started to get really weird.

About a week later I had received a comment that kind of scared me. The poster was anonymous but his comment was this, "the answer you seek is not one you want". I immediately responded and said, " you've got my attention I want to know what you know". An hour later I got another response from the same person. They said "what your referring to in your "dream" was an experiment done to certain people in which they are induced into a coma-like state where they relive their living according to what they program, they throw obstacles at you to see if you can accomplish their tasks, anyone who completes everything and gets to the age where they were subjected to the test will become".

That's when the posted ended, I began responding asking what they become, I waited 4 weeks and no response I began to get scared. I started researching about the information that was being told to me but every site with info on it was either shut down or the page was deleted. So I assumed I was fucked, but then it happened. I fell asleep that night and had the same dream but awoke to the men in lab suits speaking and what I heard was scary and unnerving " he's catching on there's a problem someone hacking in".

Then I woke up but I wasn't in my room I was in a psychiatric ward. I asked one of the staff members why I was here, he responded: " every night with you alright, look this is the last time, your parents were murdered and they're killer was never caught and you insist it was men in lab coats now goodnight". I began to panic not knowing what the hell was happening here. I took a deep breath and let go of it slowly thinking about how I could make sense of all this. I sat on the cold plastic bedding on the twin size bed in the dark, lonely room. I thought "what if I fell asleep would I wake up to my known reality?". So I began to lie down and started to drift off into a drowsy state. I was asleep and sure of it and saw once again the men in lab coats but for some strange reason, I didn't hear any noises. Then I awoke again, greeted by a voice "welcome back". I sigh with relief and say "thank god".

I felt a sense of relief knowing that one voice was assurance enough to let me know everything is going to be ok. Yet I'm not sure if that is completely true due to recent incidents that have caused a great confusion this far into this. Am I ready for what's next, or was this all a big dream from my big birthday party with all the shit I'd taken and done that night, so I ponder the thought this may be a drug-induced dream making it lucid. Who knows.

Chapter 2: Its Always Darkest Before the Dawn

I looked around shocked that my idea really worked. I looked towards the right and saw my mom in the doorway of my bedroom. I looked in her direction and said: " How long have I been out for?". She looked towards me and laughed as if I was telling a joke, "well you went to your bed around 11 o'clock last night and keep mumbling something about a test, I assumed it was about school but then you started mentioning men in lab coats I thought it was a crazy dream, so I went to my bed and woke up around 5 am and you were screaming I went in and you suddenly stopped, its 6 now so about 5 hours, honey I just wanted to know are you ok?" I looked at her and laughing in a fashion you'd see in a horror movie, replied "yeah mom, just had a bad nightmare I'm sure I'm fine everyone has one now and then" she shrugged her shoulders replying "well ok if you need to talk I'm here sweetie now get ready for school".

I got up looked around as if to let myself know everything ok it was only a dream. I walked over to the dresser to get my Beatles T-shirt and some American eagle pants, the ones that are ripped on the knee. I couldn't find my Beatles T-shirt and thought maybe it wasn't a dream due to the fact that I hadn't worn it yet because it was brand new and just put it away yesterday I ran downstairs and asked my mom "Do you know where my Beatles T-shirt is?" She looked at me like I was crazy " Beatles T-shirt? When did you get it because I don't remember you getting one" I had a confused look on my face thinking that maybe I was still asleep or maybe she just didn't remember getting it with me at Spencer's I mean it was a Beatles Revolver album cover T-shirt you don't just forget buying. I said " oh I guess I was thinking of something from my dream or something" she looked at me and shook her head and went back to drinking a cup of tea she just made and ran back upstairs and grabbed my John Lennon NYC T-shirt and walked to the shower. I turned the faucet handle and it was new looking and began thinking "when did we get this?". I brushed it off saying to myself if I keep questioning things I won't have a reality anymore. So I just thought I'll be fine I just need to see one of my friends to feel reassured.

I made it down to the bus stop 10 minutes early and just as I walked over I saw one of my friends Justin Ragni. I spend over to him hoping maybe I could talk to him about all this, I mean, after all, he's the go-to guy for these type of problems. "Justin I was wondering.... after our G.E.D classes today you think we could chill?". He looked at me in a concerted fashion and said: "sure man what's going on?". I paused trying to think of a reasonable explanation to tell him, but I couldn't at that point and time. "Well, this is going to sound a bit strange but well I have been having these weird experiences and dreams where, well I'm in a laboratory and these men in lab coats are watching from behind this enclosed room with a huge window and the last dream I had one of the men said he's not ready someone's hacking in, put him out again, Justin looked at me with a scared look as if he had just seen a ghost. "Well, man I know you think these are dreams but well there's more behind it then a simple dream, look we can't in public about this so after classes we'll meet up at my house, ok?" I looked at him worried about the statement he just made and glanced down for a minute thinking about the commenter on the forum that day when he said it was more than a dream as well. "Yeah man I appreciate it, I'm not going to lie and am pretty nervous by what you said", he looked at me and said with a stern face "Your right to feel that way".

The bus starting rolling down the hill and I began to pick up my backpack when I noticed this weird shining light coming from inside the bus. The light itself was very odd, it wasn't too bright it was actually pretty dim. Just then the bus pulled up and the light was gone, so I got in and sat all the way in the back and then I start to begin to feel a bit tired, so I rested my head on the cold metal between the seat and the interior of the bus. I began to start dosing off and that's when it happened, something I had been dreading since this all started.

I started feeling that I got when I had the first experience with the psychiatric ward I was in when I awoke the first time and yet I still feel this feeling.

When I awoke I knew what was going on from that second. It's happening again and I know where I am.

Chapter 3: The Dream Becomes A Nightmare

Again I'm here. I look around at the place I've grown to be familiar with but not happy to be in. This time around it was very different experience, there were no men in lab coats, just me laying on the cold hard metal tray that they would normally use for morgues. I had these wires attached to me still, so I began to remove them. As I removed the wires I noticed that everything began to get brighter as if the wires were like a shield hiding the true essence of the room that I had become accustomed to. I got up to start looking around when a strange voice came over a speaker somewhere in the room. " Welcome I've been waiting for you, look we don't have much time before they get back and find out what I did.". I looked around kind of confused and responded back "well I guess I don't have a choice at this point say what you need to say" my heart started racing not knowing what the hell to expect this time. "Well look you have for the past 6 years been under a psychoactive sedation drug that more or less puts you into a controllable coma state where they have you go through the obstacles they want you to, once you complete them you will be one of.... fuck I got to go we'll speak more another time." I was overcome with fear at the notion that the voice seemed as if they were about to be in a mess of trouble.

"Well hello there, why aren't you on the table?". I responded back "Look I don't know who the fuck you are or why I keep coming back to this same place every fucking time I sleep I just want some fucking answers to why the fuck I've been here for 6 years of my life, that's all I want to know and I want to go back to living a normal life and not this fucked up one you guys are creating for me". The voice laughed in a demeaning matter "Don't you remember, you wanted this and made this all possible without you this place wouldn't be what it is today". My eyes lit up in horror thinking on what was just told to me "Look I have no fucking idea what you're talking about but fuck this I'm done with this shit". I glanced over towards the enclosed room but only to find a reflection of myself and as I looked at the reflection I noticed I wasn't 19 any longer I was at least in my 40's. "Well, I'm sorry to say there is no going back you're the last of the 10 people, but I digress I'll make it simple for you, you're not leaving this place until you finish".

I began to get furious and that's when 4 men came in all in hazmat suits. I looked at them knowing what my fate was.

"You can't do this forever I will get out of here you son of a bitch" just as I finished that sentence that's when the men grabbed me and all I remember was a sharp pain in my neck as if they stuck me with a needle. I began to get woozy then eventually I passed out. That's when it started again.

This time around I didn't feel right, something was wrong. Knowing what would happen would be a much-needed blessing at this time. An I hope I get that soon or I'm not sure if I'll ever is ok. This time I hope I get needs what to be done to finish and yet I'm scared to know what is the real truth and answers in all of this bullshit.

Chapter 4: The Nightmare Begins

I woke up to the sounds of chimes from a bell. I looked towards the right and notice a church with a church bell ringing loudly, indicated it was time for mass. I got up but I wasn't at my mom's house I was in my apartment I rented when I was 18 and I wasn't quite sure what was going to happen this time. I walked around my room and seems as if I had just moved in.

I remember around this time when I was moving in Justin was going to come by and visit, so I waited for him to open the door and surprise me. He was always the type of guy to surprise me to make me happy. Just as I was thinking about that I realized I had a black suit on, as if I just came from a funeral or going to one. Right then I received a call "Chris where are you?" I was confused "Why what's wrong?" there was a pause on the phone like I had just disrespected the person on the phone "Well I figured since your supposedly Justin's friend you'd be here after what happen".

I sat down in terror hoping she wasn't saying what I think she was saying "Look I'm not feeling right today can you remind what happened?" She sighed in a slow manner as if what she was going to tell me was going to crush my heart "Don't you remember anything, Justin died in a car crash you we're in the crash you survived with minor injuries, and Justin well this is hard to say...." I looked around in sorrow knowing what I was being told and responded "please tell me I need to know" I started to hear her crying softly over the phone "He was driving and you guys we're drunk and high and he crashed into a light post and his seat belt held him but his head went through the windshield and decapitated his head" all I heard after that was her crying severely and I couldn't figure out a way to comfort her.

       I started going into shock after hearing all of this, this was a way too much for me to handle with everything I've been going through. "Look everything is going to be ok we'll get through this, Justin was a great person and I have to man up and take the blame for all of this I shouldn't have let him drive and now life is worthless,

I chose drugs over a friend and I don't deserve to live with what I have done" there was a silent pause and then she hung up. The fact that I am being thrown into all of these situations was hard enough but to lose a lifelong friend due to stupidity is one thing I cannot handle. I looked around once more and notice a letter unopened from Justin.

I sat there for a minute just looking at the name on the letter, thinking back on all the shit we did together and now all I'm left with is memories of a past paradise. So I sat and began to wonder why if there was a God why would they make someone go through these horrible experiences, did God create us because there was a flaw in himself and he couldn't feel emotion so he created us so he could try to learn emotion?

Again I'm sitting rambling to myself nothing but unanswerable questions that I may never find out. The fact of even knowing I lost someone or more or less everything in a blink of an eye and I don't even know what, why or who is doing this but I will find out and when I do they'll pay for the death of my friend, even if they just fabricated it, the fact I still can actually feel the emotion I'm going through, which by the way would be as if you saw your friend get shot and did nothing to stop when you could. You may never know what this feels like I hope you never do. The feeling is the darkest feeling you could possibly think of and I wish that on no person, not even on my worst enemies. I kept perfectly still thinking about everything that just seemed to happen for no reason at all. Looking down at the letter, I noticed that there was a broken picture with a little bit of blood as if someone had just punched it out of rage. I looked at the photo and realized it was me and Justin back in Haver Middle School and a strange sense of relief with a little bit of depression came over me as if to say soon this will be done and you'll see the people who have caused you this pain. To an equal extent, I felt the depression because how do I know they didn't fabricate this event, I mean my whole look on reality at this point is diminishing to the where I may never know what is real or not again.

As I began looking at the letter again, I realized this may be the one message he left me to help me out and I damn sure am not going to stop fighting this battle. I sighed in a sort of nostalgic manner, recalling all of the crazy shit me and Justin went through and now.... well, I'm left with just the reminisce of yesteryear and nothing good in my eyes to look forward to. I rubbed my finger's over the name on the card as if to say my last and final goodbye not knowing what the future holds in store for me next. I slid my finger under the back flap of the envelope. I began opening the letter and was hoping for some information to help me out of this mess, instead I got this confusing message "When you awake to go towards the hall near the room with the big open window, right then and there I should be working on a computer I won't have much time before they realize I have done this but please trust me to go there I'll be waiting there". I kept reading the letter over and over again to see if I can get any ideas, I mean was he speaking of a video game or my dreams. I wasn't too sure so I said well I don't have a video console so it can in my mind mean only one thing the dreams.

So as I laid down on my bed with the letter in hand a lot of things began going through my mind. Why was I the one going through all of this and not someone else? Do I have to wonder what they meant by I am the reason this is all possible? So many questions and not any answers to them. That's when I decided it would be best if maybe I just laid down and try to go through what I have been, hoping maybe just maybe I might be able to stop all of this finally.

Chapter 5: The Day Breaks

I began to feel drowsy with the notion of hoping to see my friend once again. Laying down I starting drifting more and more off into a R.E.M. mode, I felt as if I had just taken 20 Xanax Bars and 3 80 mg OxyContin's and snorted 4 huge rails of coke all at once. That's when it began to start becoming more apparent that this was an induced state of consciousness. Starting to drifting off I felt as if there would be an answer and though I may be parted but there is still a chance I can finally let it be. That's the song that kept playing in my head was "Let It Be" but I felt it was the wrong song to be stuck in my head, I felt as if the song should have been "Happiness is A Warm gun" due to the fact that I felt estranged from the emotions that I had at the time. Beginning to drift off into the unknown land I have been going to for a long time, to be honest it has felt like years when it's probably been nothing more than a couple of weeks, months, shit I'm not sure what the fuck to think anymore.

I woke up in the lab once again, remembering what was written and left for me. I just wanted answers, so I began remembering the letter and the message and starting walking out of the lab and surprisingly no men in lab coats this time. As I exited the room I noticed the room Justin was referring to so I preceded to the room with caution. When I had gotten to the door I saw a couple of weird looking laptops. I looked to the right in the window and saw Justin on the computer and preceded to walk-in. I was very nervous for the fact I didn't know what I was getting myself into. I walked in a cautious state thinking they're maybe something that I'd feared from the beginning. The same question I kept repeating to myself "Do I want to know what reality is anymore?". So far this entire journey has been a cluster fuck of disaster with a sprinkle of chaos and a dash of torment on my soon to be rested soul.

I opened the door with the confidence that I'd be ok at the end of all this. I held my breath and prepared for the worst. As soon as I walked in I saw Justin and right away said "Ok you said you didn't have much time what's the plan and what the hell is going on". A dead silence swept the room. "Well for one I'm not exactly who you think I am, look am going to be brief, My name is Michael Nurmac, I am an intelligence agent for this company before I go any further though I'm going to explain a little you are the creator of this place and I was told as was everybody we were not under any circumstances to help nor resuscitate you back to this state of conscientiousness, your mission you set for yourself was to see if people could relive events of their life but with minor adjustments the problem was that the people who took control after you went under decided that idea wasn't what they wanted, so instead they developed a new idea, one where the subjects would relive their life's but with major obstacles such as friends dying and other such things to see if you could cope with the obstacles and anyone who completed the tasks to the controllers liking was assigned a position in the New World's Army" "Look that's all I can say before we get caught just know in these "Dreams" The one person who seems to be a bit weirder then usually is me especially if they know what you're talking about, OK?" "Alright so what should I do now?" "Just go with the flow". "What does that mean?" "Look I can't explain any further, just go back into the room you were in and lie down and go back in, it'll be over soon"

I looked in horror thinking why the fuck would I go back in if I'm out, we'll some questions are better left unasked. I proceeded back into the room. "Ok now lie down and I'll put you under" "ok then what?". He was silent then I heard a faint whisper saying "it's almost over".

Chapter 6: The Tides Have Changed

As I was lying on the cold metal table I begin to be more confident in my journey to finally get this over with. I began to close my eyes in a calm fashion, thinking on everything that has happened thus far. Starting to feel the warm pressure on my chest I could feel the sedative medication doing its job. "I'm here", that's all I remember saying to myself trying to reassure myself that soon enough I'll be in another part of my past memories to get done with this whole deeply plotted plan that went horribly wrong. I remember my eyes closing and then just waking up as if I had closed them for a brief second. Looking around I starting to figure out that I was in the town Letch worth. I started thinking and as I look on the ground there was a piece of broken mirror. Looking in the mirror I saw a reflection of myself and realized I was 17 again, this was around the time where I had started doing ghost hunting with friends and I had stopped going here because one night I had a terrifying experience. I was walking in the closed down abandoned facility there and I was in the morgue, I was by myself and the rest of my friends were scattered throughout the building I began to feel a dark presence behind me as I turned around I saw a very dark menacing figure coming towards all's I remember is passing out and waking up near my friends screaming in terror.

As I was remembering all of this I heard my friend Jenna say "What's wrong Chris not getting good vibes?" reluctant to answer the question I responded "Well, to be honest, no, I'm not really feeling too good" she looked at me confused as if I was possessed by something. "Well Chris I don't get it, you called us all here to go ghost hunting, I mean we've been doing this for like 2 years straight now what the hell changed?" I looked around thinking how I could even try to begin to explain everything going on but at that point the only answer I could give was "Hey look people change and I mean we're older now if you only knew what I've been going through or what I know you wouldn't want to go in there either". We both stared at each other in a shocked manner due to the fact that we have never argued about much of anything like this, then tension finally broke "Chris out of all the years I have known you, you have never acted like this I mean what's going on you can tell me you can trust me" I was very confused at this point did the scientist hear the conversation I had when I had woken up in the lab and started talking to normal? So many questions were running through my mind at this point so I said to myself fuck it what do I have to lose?

Sweat was running down my face out of anxiety "Look if I explain this to you promise me you won't look at me differently, ok?" she looked scared I could tell. She looked at me and gave me the sign as to let me know it's ok I'm here for you. I looked at her forming thoughts in her head like I was a mad scientist. "Ever since I was 5 years old I always had this dream that felt real where I'd wake up in a lab type place in the future and when I turn 19 I have the dream but after having this dream I realized it was all true, I talked to this guy who was one of the people who helped put me under for this operation that I evidently has formed, but the people who took control after I had gone wanted to do something different with my work now I'm going through all of this nonsense for them re amusement, well that's all I know at this point" a sudden silence swept the area and Jenna began to look at me like I was crazy and needed help. She began to get a little nervous I could tell "Look Chris, I don't want to sound mean but I think you need help, look I'm going to call your mom, you should head over to the crisis center they really do help" now I started thinking why I even said anything "Look if it'll make you feel better to go ahead, I know I'm not crazy and that this is all true and if you can't take my word as a friend of 10 plus years then I guess we really shouldn't be friends". She looked at me in amazement that I even conjured up those words I just violently threw at her brain. "Chris out of all the years I've known you I can honestly say you are at your lowest point and I can't be anywhere near you when you realize you're fighting a war with your mind and you're not going to win, so why don't you just give up and go along with it?". I sat there thinking why this sounds odd and then it hit me that wasn't Jenna it was one of them. "Look Jenna just call my mom I'm out of here I'm going to go to Crisis, and before I go, just answer me one thing Why?". She looked at me in a stern fashion and replied "You did this to yourself we had no part" the minute she said that I began realizing that all of the people in this hallucination or virtual world are in actuality the people controlling this whole experiment and they wanted nothing more than to hurt my progress on fixing this mess, but I won't let them do that I have too much at stake.

Right then my mom pulled up in her town and country van looking busted like I remembered. She looked at me as she pulled close and yelled "GET IN THIS DAMN CAR NOW' I looked at her as if to say seriously is in a supposed crisis and your yelling? "Alright Mom is coming now ok?" she looked at me furiously and nodded. I waved goodbye to "Jenna" for a reason only I'll understand. The entire car ride we were silent and didn't even look in each other's direction. We finally got to the Crisis Center and then things became a little bit druggy feeling as if I had been drugged. I turned around and there were the men in lab coats, going down I turned towards my Mom and said help but all she said was "It's for the best sweetie trust me". I began to have a panic attack not knowing what was going to happen to me at that point and time but at the same token I didn't care any longer it was just too much stress to think on where I was going to be next. That's the exact minute I passed out. "Well, you think he'll find out soon that he won't win?" "I can't say for certain he has someone helping him and apparently they know where we're going to be so there's no telling what could happen we just got to watch him closer is all" "Yes Sir". (Blackness)

Chapter 7: The Recurring Thought

And Dr. Dre said, "Slim Shady you a base head" Uh, uhh, So why's your face red? Man you wasted Well, since age twelve, I've felt like I'm someone else 'Cause I hung my original self from the top bunk with a belt". That was the song I heard playing as I awoke from what felt like hours of sleep. I opened my eyes in shock to see where I was at. I was at the beginning of this whole journey back at the day it started, my 19th birthday. It was morning still so I hadn't done anything yet, what were they trying to have me do? what was going to happen now? all these questions running through my head and yet I can't find myself one true answer. I Got out of my bed and threw on some jeans that were on the ground. I walked over towards my laptop to turn off the song and the song starts getting distorted and the last lyrics it shreds out is "Stop the tape! This kid needs to be locked away! (Get him!) Dr. Dre, don't just stand there, OPERATE! I'm not ready to leave, it's too scary to die (Fuck that!), Tell him that I slit his throat, in this dream I had". I began to get scared thinking maybe someone was planting a message in the song to watch out for something, but what?

I Threw a shirt on and just shook off the entire thought of it being subliminally implanted into my thoughts. Walking down the stairs I started to feel as if this wasn't my apartment. As if something was missing and that's when it hit me like a ton of bricks, where's my roommate? The day of my birthday in the morning my roommate was lying on the couch and well had woken up to me running down the stairs in a very anxious manner that of a 5-year-old on Christmas morning running to the tree for the presents. Oddly enough it seemed as if I never had a roommate. I began thinking to myself I can't have friends or even roommates am I destined to stay lonely in this pathetic excuse of an experimental dream gone wrong and constantly rearranging the life I had already come accustom to? Why the fuck did I have to think of such an idea if that's what actually fucking happened, I mean if I'm that smart in the future why didn't I think this was a plausible outcome once I went under? I began to just think for a second it doesn't matter I'll never be able to change the past by constantly trying to find answers to my own questions. I just stopped thinking about that all and got back onto the track to find out what the fuck happened to my roommate if I did have one.

I walked outside my apartment building thinking about how any of this could by far get any stranger and unnerving than it already is. My head was still on the thought of the theory about the screwed up song that was messing up as I woke, I mean is it possible it was a message or a coincidence that I just happened to wake up when my computer just started lagging whilst on the song. All these questions and no answers, Again back at square one. Standing outside, the apartment I began to see if there was any way to get answers by getting any ordinary information that I knew vs the new information being told in the new memory being recreated. The first idea that popped into my never ending mindless thought process was to let me just ask the apartment tenant if they know where my roommate may be at. Starting to walk to the door I noticed that my tenant's name was missing from the bell service we had that buzzed people into the building. So I buzzed 4A my next door neighbors to see if they knew what number the tenant's apartment is and for that matter who is the tenant, "Buzz, Buzz, Buzz, Crackle" "Hello, can I help you?" "Yes I'm looking for the tenant of the building" " Yea no problem his apartment number is 4 B his Names Chris here I'll buzz you in" (Buzz, unlocking of a door), I couldn't believe what I just heard, I'm the tenant?

There had to be some mistake there's no way that I'm the tenant. I walked up to the elevator and pushed for the 4th floor. It stopped at the 3rd floor to let someone in, it was a man with a trench coat maybe in his 30's late 30's with a brown fedora. I look him up and down and he turns to me and in a deep scratchy voice muttered lowly "Soon it will be done, Soon". It hit the 4th floor and I got off and turned back only to notice no man there. What the fuck is going on here? I got to my apartment and walked to the door slowly and looked at the name on the door and below it read "TENANT". My heart dropped into my stomach not knowing what year nor what the hell was going on. I unlocked my door, walked to my bed and sat down for second holding my head with my hands. What am I going to do? Who can even help me? They can't break me. Thinking on all of that I came to the conclusion that well I should just go to sleep and finish this, wake up in the lab, stay awake without getting drugged and take back control. The fight may have been started by them but I'm going to be the one to finish it with victory in my mind, soul, and heart even if I die trying to win, I will succeed in my own mind, I'll die for a better future for others, to not endure what I am for the government. It ends now.

Chapter 8: All Is Fair in Love and War

All is fair in love and war, but in this situation, all is fair in war. Lying down I began forming a plan of action to help me succeed once I woke up in the lab. Starting to drift into a horrifying feeling of fear mixed with sadness, I felt soon I'll be done with this all. What else could I do at this point anyway, I've come this far at least I think I have.

Lying there I realized I was beginning to start to fall asleep. Feeling everything starting to get lighter, I knew I'll be asleep. Blackness starts to surround every inch of my room. I knew what was next.

A flash of light exploding in front of me. I was here and very aware I was. I started ripping off the wires attached to me and it began getting brighter, I scurried off the table and raced to the door. (loudspeaker crackles) "you thought it would be that easy?" As I turned the knob I realized it was locked. "I didn't take the moment to think of a plan but since it's not that easy why don't you make this a little harder? Why fuck with me why not let me just figure it out?" a pause " but you have". A sudden feeling of pressure pushing on my chest is what I felt after hearing that, "what the fuck did I figure out? Nothing, that's what. I'm not sure where you getting your damn information from but it sure as hell isn't correct" laughter is all I heard for the next 2 minutes. (Loudspeaker crackles) " well my source is very reliable I assure you, I'm pretty sure you know him". Beginning to get annoyed at the whole conversation I figured might as well ask some questions. As I clear my throat I begin to formulate some questions in my mind " Look I just want to know the whole story if that's ok with your plan"

   (Crackle) " Well sounds reasonable to me I will come and meet you down there". Hearing footsteps walking downstairs I felt I might have just majorly screwed myself badly. The door began to open in a slow agonizing fashion. My heart starts pounding like that of a scared child in a haunted house. The door opens and my heart drops into my stomach. It's been him all along and I never knew. No wonder he wasn't around all those years.

Chapter 9: Love Means War

Looking around as if I had just been pranked. I wasn't sure how to handle anything about this whole situation. " so, you aware of my informant yet or should I tell you?" I stood astonished my own family member against me, I can honestly say I wouldn't have saw this coming at all. Grasping for what little air I had left in my frozen lungs, I ask the one question I had since I was a child, where were you? He stood there and said with a slight depressing tone " The one who does without his entire life learns true happiness, one who is more fortunate learns true sadness." Looking at him as if he was Nostradamus I replied " so you did without me and what true happiness did you gain?" Leisurely he responded " all of this, including seeing you and all your troubles,

in a sense I've always been there, son."
Stunned by the response I stood there in a
state of shock thinking on how fucked up
his mind has gotten from all this bullshit
with these experiments , one remark came
to thought " So, you feel you've justified not
being in my life from childhood till now by
thinking all you had to do to fix a huge
problem was speaking in quotes to try and
make me think it was for the better? you
must be out of your god damn mind to
believe for one millisecond that I would
accept that as a sorry like you did nothing
wrong, your pathetic and a sorry excuse for
a father , son and human being and should
be ashamed for what you put me through
to just get rid of all the guilt you have, that
is if you even can comprehend what guilt is
or if you even feel guilty , you disgust me".

   At that point I looked him sternly in his
eyes with a look of disbelief seeing that he
felt he did what needed to be done and
feels he made up for the lost time from my
childhood and up. "Well, Son it's hard to
explain why everything I just said is true,

look I'll try my best to help you understand why what I said should forgive everything you feel I did not provide for you all those years that have past, if it'll make you know then I feel it'll make you feel differently about this entire situation". Feeling as if there wasn't any possible way he could encourage me to change my opinion and feelings towards my father or should I say my ghost of a father. He began to clear his throat in such a fashion as if what he was going to say would answer and explain everything I wanted to know and what I needed to hear. Looking directly in his eyes he began " It started when you were born, I at the time was a Scientist Working with the Government at a base well known by the public due to U.F.O conspiracies, to us it's called groom lake section 3 grid map 2 level 01, to most it is known as Area 51, Being well known for my work on experiments of Mind manipulation as well as memory manipulation to change past events to what we needed to implement our own obstacles as a test of strength, will and determination to complete all of the obstacles, the goal in the end of the experiment was to create the best soldier ever created, one without emotion to be able to follow through with orders most soldiers wouldn't do for the main fact that they had a conscience something that the experiment would remove from the subject, the plan was to eliminate any emotion and conscience from the subject to do what needed to be done, the problem was we accomplished what we wanted but at a cost, the soldiers wouldn't listen to the orders given because somewhere in our calculations we messed up and created a human less psychopath that wanted nothing more than to murder for the sake to figure what was reality and what was fabricated by us, in short I recruited you my son knowing that you had the will power and smarts but the experiment was breach by a unknown person who messed up the work we've been doing and now you're in sorts not sure what is and is not real the fabrications are some mixed up with the real past that you'll always be questioning your own reality which is why I told every worker not to revive you to a conscience state due to this very problem and at this point and time there is not a way to fix nor reverse the damage, believe me son my intentions were good but my downfall was trusting workers I personally don't know and can't trust, I know you have a lot of questions you want answers to, so with that being said ask what you need to ask and I'll answer them as much as I can."

Completely unexpected is what I was thinking in my head, he did what I thought he could not which was to explain in full what happened but as for forgiveness he won't be receiving any from for the fact that he couldn't even apologize for everything he's done. Knowing that there wasn't much else to ask but one thing "Why?" he stared emotionless into my glassy eyes filled with an array of different emotions "I did what I thought was best for you and the family". For the family really that's the only line he could muster up as a response. I guess I was hoping he would have something more meaningful to say as if it would make the pain go away from all of the these but no. I began just trying to piece all of these together when it hit me. This isn't it, this is only the beginning. I knew it just then I could feel it and I knew exactly what was going to happen, and it did.

Boom, the only sound at first that I heard along other noises that crept in after the loud boom. I'm her, this is just grand. "Chris man you need to chill out bro, I mean I know it's your birthday but I'm not trying to get arrested on your birthday. Get home dude.". Fuck I knew this was going to happen why, why couldn't it just stop after that last somewhat meaningful conversation. "Yea no problem I see ya soon" playing it off but damn what am I going to do this is getting way out of hand. I began walking to my car, taking the keys out of my jacket I started to feel as if all this shit wasn't over. Got my keys out and unlocked my car door, getting inside I got this strange sense of relaxation mixed with fear. Just put the key in the ignition and go is what I kept saying to myself to make sure I didn't just sit there the entire time. Finally, after about 10 seconds of sitting I started the car, I pulled out and started making my way home. ring, ring, ring, "Hello?" "Chris you need to get out, please stop whatever you're doing and go to your apartment" "Who is this this?" pause "It doesn't matter just go" dial tone was all I heard she had just hung up.

I made my way home and raced up the stairs to my apartment, but why? I unlocked my door, only to find everything was in place, why was I rushed here so fast. RIIIIINNG RIIIIING RIIIING [New Text Message from Unknown] I opened my phone the minute I saw it and I saw something that would scare me to death. "Chris you need to fall asleep all you just went through was fake this what I am telling you is real please for your sake and live fall asleep". I rushed to my bed, I took a Xanax and Ambien and hoped for the best. I began feeling the effects of the medications, they were moving in quick. I was asleep.

Chapter 10: Dead End

Ok now, what do I do I'm right back where I began. Nothing seems as if anything is going to change, I mean honestly what do I have to do to be done with this all? Answerless questions I still ask myself to this very moment. The entire time I was wondering who the damn person on the phone was, and what did they mean? Feeling the intense pressure building up on my chest, I realized after everything I just went through all those times I woke up in the lab, they were all fabrications as well. Thinking on that I wondered if the same can be said about the encounter with my father, is he really that deranged? It was happening and I could feel it I was going to wake up soon to this bullshit comedy sketch show which now is my life.

I started waking up I knew it was time and when I did I began to get scared, Where's the lab? I woke up to a nice house lying next to a woman and in the background, I could hear kids yelling in excitement. What day is it and where am I? That's all I wanted to know and I began to figure it out. It's Christmas Day, but I'm not sure where I am yet. As I'm figured all of this out I noticed the woman waking up "Merry Christmas Honey" what the hell is going on here, now I have a wife? trying to figure out what's going on I say "Morning Beautiful how'd you sleep?" she began yawning and stretching her arms "Well I had a wonderful night last night it's nice that your parents have the kids for the weekend" kids? seriously, I myself still am a kid and couldn't fathom the thought, not that I don't like kids but I mean I didn't even experience life yet and now I own a house have kids and a wife, what else am I going to run into. Waking up I got out of the bed and stretched, beginning to try to do a what I would probably normally do.

I found my dresser and got some clothes and proceeded to the shower. As I was going to get in I noticed that the knob on the shower looked just like the one I saw at the beginning of all this when I was at my mom's, what the fuck is with this shit. "Honey, do you know where my keys are?" thinking of what I might normally say "No, I thought you had put them up last night?" feeling scared thinking maybe she might think I'm sick or something for fear of being brought to the hospital I had to play everything right "I guess I did, I found them they were in the dresser drawer". I turned the knob and the water began pouring over me then I began to feel weird. Getting out of the shower I noticed everything was getting strange, everything just felt off like I was fucked up on salvia. Walking to the door I heard a scream, I ran into my room and saw no one, then I saw it. It was a white light just in the bathroom similar to the one I saw on the bus that day. The door began opening and when it did the light dimmed and out came this man who looked like he could possibly be my real father. He starts walking out "Christopher, look a lot of stuff is happening right now and I know you don't know what real or not but listen I know it's hard but always imagine something that makes you feel good and I guarantee that light will shine and I will be there" deep words from a person I barely know and yet it's like he's a family member in a strange way. He told me to sit down we needed to talk.

The man began staring at me and said "I'm someone you know and I care about you deeply, I know you may not know me or even believe me with all of this but there's some things I need to tell you, but before I can you need to go to sleep in order to wake up and ill help you but you have to trust me" Wow in a sort of emotional manner I began to get teary eyed knowing real or not someone cares about me and that was one thing I wanted from the beginning "Ok I trust you, what do I get to do?". He explained to me in manner as if was a soldier going into combat "You need to go to sleep to be awake and in order to do that we need to get to the source, which is a man of great power in the new world military, we have to get you back to the one memory were you two first met and we will be done" thinking on how easy it was I responded "Ok so you just want me to go to sleep?" he nodded.

Laying down I realized he's my father, he's got to be. Feeling the intense heat and pressure on my chest I knew it was only a matter of time before I would be going to another memory again. Which one is the question I kept thinking the entire time? It was beginning to get darker, and evil feeling in the room, but why? I was under and knew it, but why wasn't I waking up, what the fuck is going on now? Am I stuck in the in-between? did I die? I don't know but it sure as hell was scary. Then I began to see some light, I go into my new memory and it didn't feel bad but I was so wrong. Waking up I saw nothing but black, dark clouds outside where am I. A man at that moment walks into what I think is a room is in "Sir, the enemies are pushing the front we need more weapons and men, Sir" No damn no, this can't be happening. What did I do, it's all over I know it is! This was the moment I was dreading from the beginning. The new world is here and humans aren't the only beings here anymore.

Made in the USA
Columbia, SC
28 November 2018